Dear Parents and Educators,

Welcome to Penguin Young Readers! As parents and educators, you know that each child develops at his or her own pace—in terms of speech, critical thinking, and, of course, reading. Penguin Young Readers recognizes this fact. As a result, each Penguin Young Readers book is assigned a traditional easy-to-read level (1–4) as well as a Guided Reading Level (A–P). Both of these systems will help you choose the right book for your child. Please refer to the back of each book for specific leveling information. Penguin Young Readers features esteemed authors and illustrators, stories about favorite characters, fascinating nonfiction, and more!

Peter Rabbit™ Best Bunnies	LEVEL 2
	GUIDED READING LEVEL I

This book is perfect for a **Progressing Reader** who:
- can figure out unknown words by using picture and context clues;
- can recognize beginning, middle, and ending sounds;
- can make and confirm predictions about what will happen in the text; and
- can distinguish between fiction and nonfiction.

Here are some **activities** you can do during and after reading this book:
- Character Traits: Come up with a list of words to describe Peter and Benjamin. How are these two characters different?
- Make Predictions: At the end of the story, Peter Rabbit says that going into the garden is dangerous, but we know that he will go again. What do you think will happen next time he goes? Discuss how you would continue the adventures of Peter Rabbit.

Remember, sharing the love of reading with a child is the best gift you can give!

Sarah Fabiny
Editorial Director
Penguin Young Readers program

D0062467

*Penguin Young Readers are leveled by independent reviewers applying the standards developed by Irene Fountas and Gay Su Pinnell in *Matching Books to Readers: Using Leveled Books in Guided Reading*, Heinemann, 1999.

PENGUIN YOUNG READERS
An Imprint of Penguin Random House LLC

Published in the United States of America in 2018 by Penguin Young Readers, an imprint of
Penguin Random House LLC, 345 Hudson Street, New York, New York 10014.

Manufactured in China

ISBN 9780241331583

10 9 8 7 6 5 4 3 2 1

PENGUIN YOUNG READERS

LEVEL **2**
PROGRESSING
READER

BEST BUNNIES

Penguin Young Readers
An Imprint of Penguin Random House

This is Peter Rabbit.

Peter lives with his three
sisters, Flopsy, Mopsy,
and Cotton-tail.

Flopsy likes to dance.
Mopsy likes to sew.
Cotton-tail wants to go into
Mr. McGregor's garden, but
Peter does not think it is safe.

Their cousin, Benjamin,
also lives with them.
Benjamin is a bit clumsy,
but is very smart and wise.

Peter gets into trouble,
but is good inside.
Peter and Benjamin are
best friends.

The bunnies live near
Mr. McGregor's garden.
It is very pretty with lots
of fruits and vegetables.

Mr. McGregor does not like the rabbits coming into the garden.

The bunnies also live near Bea's cottage.
Bea paints pictures of them.
She is their friend and tries to look after them.

One day, Peter wants to go
into the garden to eat.
He has snuck in many times
before, but this time Peter is
feeling a little scared.

Benjamin can tell his cousin is scared. Benjamin is, too, but he says, "I will go with you!"

Peter feels much better.
The cousins creep
under the gate and
into the garden.

In the garden there are
pumpkins, peas, and tomatoes.
"Look at all this tasty food!"
says Peter.
They hear someone coming.

It is Mr. McGregor!
He chases the rabbits.

Peter and Benjamin run
in and out of the pumpkins.
Then they slide under a door
and into a garden shed.
They are trapped!

Mr. McGregor is very happy and says, "I have got you now, rabbits!"
He turns the plant pots over one by one, until . . .

Hop! Peter hops from the pot and jumps back into the garden.

Mr. McGregor chases him.
But where is Benjamin?

A pot is moving through
the lettuces.
Mr. McGregor doesn't see it.
Then the pot starts running.
Benjamin is inside!

Benjamin runs for the gate.
Mr. McGregor almost
catches him!
Benjamin runs all the way
back to Bea's house.

Safe at last, Peter asks
Benjamin, "Are you okay?"

Benjamin is not happy.
"That was scary," he says.
Peter agrees.
"This time we were lucky to
get away," Peter says.

But we all know Peter will go into the garden again!